Enter the world of the sea otters.

How do they survive as mariners?

You can find them in the kelp.

They love to play, groom and yelp.

But how do they survive in water so cold?

The kelp environment can be harsh, but the otters are bold.

Every creature is part of the food chain.

Are you curious how otters thrive in their domain?

Discover the habits and menu of these furry sea mammals.

Learn of their fears as they interact with other marine animals.

Hydra and Muste otter encounter other sea creatures.

Read on to experience their thrilling adventures.

THE EXCITING ADVENTURES OF HYDRA AND MUSTE OTTER

LIFE IN THE BIG SEA

by

George Kingston

Published by G Sharp Productions
Copyright © 1999 by George Kingston

All rights reserved. Printed in the United States of America. No part of this book may be reproduced or transmitted in any form, or by any means, including electronic or mechanical via photocopying, recording, or by any information storage and retrieval system without written permission from the author, except for the inclusion of brief quotations in a review.

G Sharp Productions books may be purchased for either personal, educational, or promotional use. For information, please write

    G Sharp Productions
    220 Oak Meadow Drive
    Los Gatos, CA 95032

    or

visit the G Sharp Productions Web site at www.gsharpproductions.com

First G Sharp Productions edition published 2001.

Graphic art by Coast Engraving, Inc.

Library of Congress Control Number: 2001116578

ISBN 0-9669852-1-4

The Exciting Adventures of
HYDRA & MUSTE OTTER:
Life in the Big Sea

By George J. Kingston

G Sharp Productions

Somewhere near a slough along the jagged, cliff coastline in the Pacific Ocean, Hydra, a female sea otter floated on her back next to a giant kelp. Using her tough padded forepaws to hold a prickly, purple sea urchin, Hydra happily nibbled on it.

Her male otter friend, Muste, wrapped in a piece of kelp to keep close to Hydra, held a tasty crab on his chest. Muste ripped the crab legs off and chewed them one at a time. Next he held the body with his forepaws and used his sharp incisor teeth to crack it open. Muste then held the crab shell like a large bowl against his mouth and scraped out the delicious food.

"This purple sea urchin tastes yummy," said Hydra.

"Hydra," Muste laughing, "your mouth is so purple from eating those sea urchins!"

"Try some, Muste; all you ever eat are those crabs," squeaked Hydra.

Muste appeared thoughtful for a moment before replying, "I'm glad we each like different types of food. That way, we won't compete for the same food in my territory."

As Hydra lay back, feeling the warm sun on her face and her tummy full and content, she announced, "I really like this area. The kelp forest has tasty food and it is a great place to hide and sleep. We don't have to dive too deep to find food on the rocky bottom and we can easily swim to shore when the sea becomes too rough."

"Yes, I chose this one-half-mile spot for my home for those same reasons, Hydra. I only let friendly females like you live here with me. Other young male otters and adults can only pass through because I staked this place out as my territory," boasted Muste.

Hydra appreciated Muste's informative hospitality, but she was still hungry. She used her large, webbed hind feet and flattened tail to propel her four-foot slender, sleek body with powerful strokes through the kelp forest in search of more of her favorite food—the purple sea urchin.

Once on the ocean floor, she noticed many of them near a sea slug. Hydra grabbed the sea urchins and stored them in her loose pouch under her foreleg. She then proceeded to rapidly dig a trench with her forepaws in search of another tasty favorite she found hard to resist—clams! After energetically searching her newly created trench, she discovered three appetizing clams. Hydra added them to her pouch collection as she began to envision the bountiful feast she would enjoy, floating on her back, once she reached the surface. Planning ahead, she grabbed a rock from the bottom of the ocean to break open her tasty morsels later.

As soon as Hydra popped through the surface of the sea, she rolled onto her back, took one of the clams from her pouch and hammered it with the rock. Bang! Bang! Bang! She inspected the clamshell, but it had not cracked. After several more bangs, the shell finally broke and she gobbled down the yummy clam inside. She systematically finished off the other clams just as the first. Hydra then used the rock to crack open the purple sea urchins covered with sharp spines and briskly ate their tasty hidden morsels.

Muste, still hungry after his crab feast, dived 60 feet to the ocean bottom and found a heavy, shelled abalone attached to a rock. He tried to pull the abalone off the rock with his strong forepaws. The abalone clamped down with great force. Muste grabbed a large stone from the ocean floor with both his forepaws and bashed the side of the abalone shell with several rapid strokes. After his persistent bashing, he was able to lift the abalone from the rock.

When Muste returned to the surface, he asked Hydra, "Can I use your rock to open this stubborn abalone I just caught?" Hydra swam to him and handed Muste her rock. With his skillful paws, Muste laid the rock on his chest and smashed the abalone repeatedly on the rock until it cracked open.

"Thank you so much for loaning me your rock, Hydra," said Muste as he chewed on the abalone with delight.

Hydra asked, "Do you think it would be easier to open the abalone shell by banging the rock on it like I did with the clam?"

Muste replied, "That would work too, but I usually like to use the rock on my chest and strike the shell on top of it until it opens. It gives me more control with the larger abalone shells." Hydra appeared impressed at Muste's thoughtful skill.

With their bellies full of sea urchins, abalone, crab and clams, the otters cleaned the shells from their fur by rolling over and over in the water. They wrapped themselves in kelp before taking an afternoon nap. Muste held his forepaws and hind feet out of the water. Hydra covered her eyes with her forepaws and also raised her hind feet out of the water. As the sun warmed their faces and feet, they fell asleep.

Suddenly, Nova, the humpback whale, breached the water, splashing the peacefully sleeping otters. Startled, Hydra and Muste swam over to Nova.

"Hey, Nova, thanks for the shower," Muste and Hydra chattered sarcastically.

"Any time!" chuckled Nova, as water spouted from his blowhole. "Why did you two wrap yourselves in kelp and hold your hands and feet out of the water while you were sleeping?" the humpback whale asked curiously.

"If we wrap ourselves in kelp, we won't float away while we sleep," giggled Hydra. "You know how strong the tides and currents can be in this Pacific Ocean."

Muste added, "Our flippers and paws don't have much fur on them. The sun's rays warm them and we try to save heat in our bodies at the same time by keeping them out of the water."

"Otters are always thinking; I like that in an animal," said Nova.

"We're just trying to stay warm and survive," yipped Hydra in her squeaky little voice.

"Your bodies are so small. I have blubber to protect me from these cold Pacific waters," boasted Nova, "but how do you keep yourselves from freezing to death?"

"Well, Nova," Muste explained, "it's true we are the only marine mammal without a layer of blubber or fat, but we have two layers of dense, water-resistant fur that protect us from the cold. Humans call our long, outer fur 'guard hairs,' and this layer of our fur gives us an overall soft and fuzzy appearance. It also helps keep our inner layer, known as underfur, dry. One square inch of our underfur could have a million hairs—more than any other animal in the world."

Hydra added, "We also need to eat approximately one quarter to one third of our body weight in food every day to stay warm in this chilly water."

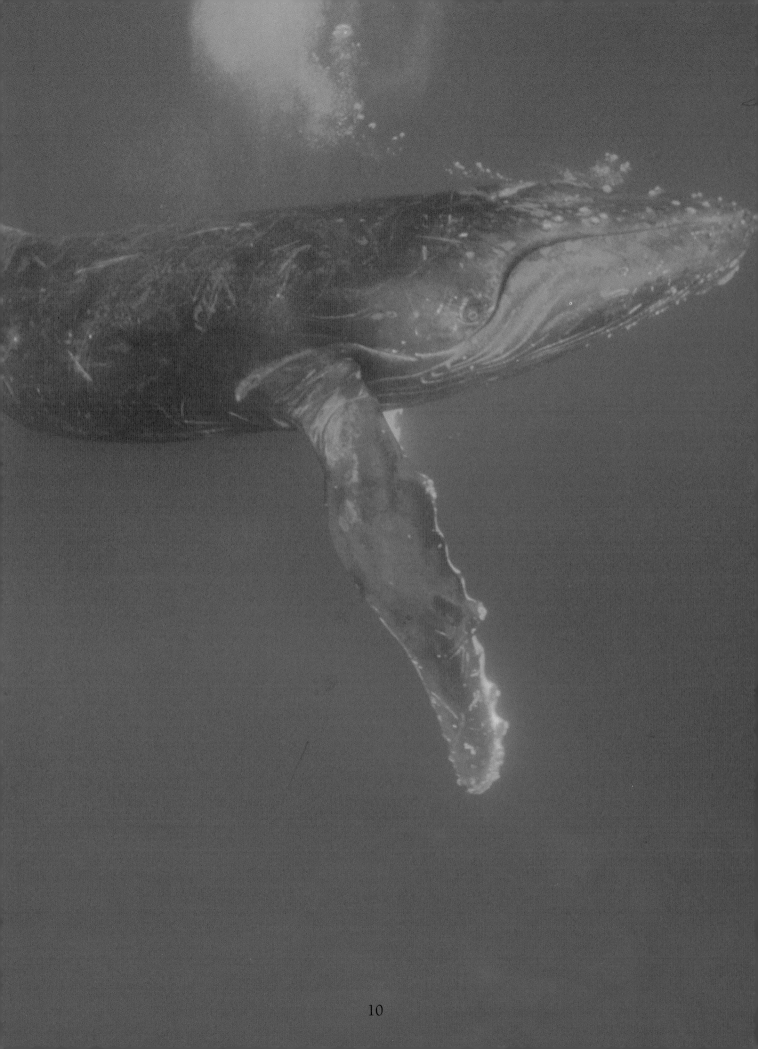

Nova asked, "Why does a lot of food keep you warm?"

"Unfortunately, the cold water rapidly draws heat out of our bodies," Muste replied. "We need to keep our body temperature close to 100 degrees Fahrenheit, which humans call 'thermoregulation.' Our bodies rapidly burn the calories we get from our food that warm us. We need to eat a lot of food so our bodies can burn the calories and also stay warm. Animals like us with high metabolic rates (which means we burn food calories quickly) need to eat a lot of food every day. Our metabolic rate is two to three times higher than that of a land mammal close to our size."

"That's a lot of clams, sea urchins and abalone every day," spouted Nova.

"We love to eat those tasty morsels, especially purple sea urchins and crabs, but mussels and those little red octopuses are yummy too. Humans call all our favorite food 'marine invertebrates.' They have lots of calories to help us stay warm," yelped Hydra.

"Gee, Nova, we've certainly seen you eat a lot of krill too," chuckled both otters as they somersaulted around the whale.

"My large body needs a lot of food. I guess both of us need to eat a lot of sea creatures to survive, even though it's for different reasons," Nova replied thoughtfully. "You know, those somersaults of yours remind me. I've noticed how all you otters are always touching your fur, rolling in the water and rubbing your fur against each other. Is this your way of grooming?" asked Nova.

"You are quite right, Nova!" squeaked Hydra.

Muste giggled as he said, "The rolling and touching fluffs up our underfur to trap tiny air bubbles between each hair. The bubbles form a protective pocket of air at the base of our underfur to keep our skin dry and us warm."

Hydra added, "Touching each other increases our skin circulation and spreads natural oils from our glands onto our skin and fur, which adds to our protection against the cold water. Besides, rolling and touching can be fun, too!" As Hydra talked, she climbed onto Nova and tickled his blowhole.

"Hey you little rascal, get off of me!" Nova spouted between uncontrollable bursts of laughter as he bobbed his giant body from side to side in the sea. Hydra slipped back into the water from Nova's back, her tummy a little upset from all the sudden rocking on a full stomach of clams. Composed again, Nova developed a puzzled look on his face and asked, "Can you touch all of your body or do you need each other to groom yourselves?"

"Because we have a really loose skeleton and fur coat and no collarbone, we have the flexibility to clean every part of our body," Hydra said as she bent her body backward into a circle to demonstrate.

"Wow, you really are flexible fur balls," Nova snorted.

"Our survival depends on our flexibility to groom every inch of hair on our body so we maintain the air pocket in our underfur, which prevents the cold water from contacting our skin," squeaked Hydra.

Muste explained further by saying, "We use our forepaws to press water out of our fur. We also rub the fur hard to get air next to the skin and finally we blow air into our thick coat, which traps the air in our underfur. Since our fur is loose on our bodies, we can pull on it to bring hard-to-reach areas closer. We roll, twist and squirm until every square inch of our fur is groomed. A good final shake leaves our fur remarkably dry."

"We always groom after eating and when we wake up," Hydra said.

"We also scrub, lick and comb our fur," yipped Muste as he showed Nova his grooming forepaws, sporting short claws he could partially retract.

"If our fur is not cleaned and becomes matted, the air bubbles escape and the cold water touches our skin, which reduces heat in our bodies. If our bodies lose too much heat, we will die," whimpered Hydra.

Muste climbed on top of the huge whale and mischievously tapped his blowhole.

"You little rascals get off me," bellowed Nova, creating a water gush that pushed Muste back into the sea, "or I'll swallow you the way I do my herring!"

"You must really like herring," teased Hydra.

"You bet I do. Every year my whale friends and I migrate north to Alaska just for the herring," said Nova as his one eye that Hydra and Muste could see, took on a dreamy look.

"How do you catch them?" asked the otters in unison.

"We chase a school of herring and herd them into a circle by blowing bubbles around them that creates a *bubble net*," Nova explained. "The herring get so confused by our bubble net, they swim closer and closer to the surface. Then all we have to do is open our mouths and devour tons of herring," Nova gurgled enthusiastically as he demonstrated the feeding position in the water.

"Wow, that's good fishing," Hydra said with admiration.

"Thank you," Nova replied with a glint of pride in his eye.

Muste changed the subject as he asked a burning question. "We heard the otters in Alaska can form 'rafts' of up to 2,000 otters at a time." He and Hydra grabbed Nova's tubercles and climbed back up onto his back, eagerly awaiting his answer.

Nova spurted, almost knocking the otters off him with a strong stream of water from his blowhole. "I understand that two or more otters together form a raft. You and Hydra would be considered a raft, is that right?" he asked.

"Yes," Hydra answered. "Did you learn about rafts from those Alaskan otters?"

"I certainly spoke to them," Nova replied. "One otter raft I swam into must have had 2,000 otters. They were very curious about me. Those otters had so much energy—and enormous appetites like the two of you." The playful otters somersaulted backward and suddenly found themselves balanced between the great flukes of the whale's tail.

"Nova, could you give us a whale-tail-sail?" they asked eagerly.

Bubbling his agreement, Nova slapped his great big pectoral fin on the water. With a quick flick of his tail, the otters flew over him, splashing into the kelp. Hydra and Muste had a great time climbing back onto Nova and sailing through the air over and over. Nova enjoyed playing with the otters as well.

He laughed and said, "You fur balls are a lot of fun. By the way, I think I should warn you. I recently heard from my whale friends that Carcha, the great white shark, is lurking in these waters. I understand one in ten otters become a snack for great white sharks. You two would make tasty snacks."

"Thank you for warning us, Nova. We'll watch for that white beast of terror," Hydra said shivering.

"Yes, you be careful," Nova replied as he started to swim away.

"Nova," Muste called to the departing whale, "are you going to enter the talent show? The winner receives a year's supply of his favorite fish."

"Thank you for reminding me. It should be lots of fun," Nova called back. Blowing geyserlike waterspouts in the air, Nova slowly cruised down the coastline, singing his favorite songs, searching for krill and daydreaming about his act for the big talent show.

Humpback Whale Songs

Spout, spout; watch the water fly high!

Here comes that humpback cruising by.

Out from the water, the mighty whale breaches.

Splash, splash; look how far he reaches!

Listen to the sounds, so mystic to the ear.

Squeak, squeal, and whistle; maybe another whale will appear.

The melody will travel such a long way, searching for a date,

With hopes of reaching a beautiful mate.

How the humpback loves to eat krill,

And loves to catch herring with such bubbling skill.

Humpback whale songs so beautiful to hear,

They represent life that will always persevere.

Nova's warning caused Hydra and Muste to be nervous about Carcha, the hungry white shark. The otters kept a continuous check on the water below them. They watched a giant manta ray flapping its huge wings. "Could that be Biros gliding through the water?" they wondered. A blue shark slowly meandered away in the opposite direction. If Carcha should be sighted, the otters agreed they would hide in the protective kelp fronds.

"It's safe here, and I'm hungry again," announced Muste. "Let's go find something to eat." As they dived towards the ocean bottom, Muste noticed something in the distance moving in their direction. Whatever was swimming toward them was too big to be another otter, too small to be another Nova and too fast for a manta ray. Frightened, Muste motioned to Hydra to hide behind a large kelp stalk.

Suddenly, out of the water jumped Bottlenose, the dolphin. He chattered at the otters, "Eek, eek, were you playing hide and seek with me?" "I had both of you echolocated long ago," boasted Bottlenose.

"What does 'echolocated' mean, Bottlenose?" asked the puzzled otters, peeking from the protection of the kelp.

"It means I send out clicking sounds that bounce off objects like you, fish and the surrounding terrain and come back to me as an echo. A special receiver in my ear sends the echo signals to my brain, which determines how far away any object is, its position and size or an overall picture of what's around me. So I knew you were here long before I could see you," explained Bottlenose.

"Well for now, be quiet, Bottlenose!" Hydra squealed.

"We heard a rumor from Nova that Carcha could be prowling these waters. We don't want her to hear you!" squeaked Muste.

"Is that mean, nasty white shark causing problems around here again? I haven't felt her vibrations around these waters lately. Eek, eek, eek, she doesn't scare me. I'll just bop her with my nose," chattered Bottlenose.

"But she is huge and always hungry," Hydra said.

Muste added, "She devours all kinds of sea mammals like elephant seals, sea lions and even dolphins. You can never tell when she's about to eat you until it's too late because she likes to swim near the bottom with her countershaded gray and white body, darting to the surface for a tasty meal. Carcha is one stealthy shark!"

Bottlenose replied, a little nervously now, "I didn't know she had grown so much and had such a big appetite." "But Carcha likes to eat animals with lots of blubber so you shouldn't worry," Bottlenose added reassuringly. Nevertheless, Hydra and Muste believed Carcha would eat anything and decided to stay close to the kelp forest.

"After I echolocated you, I noticed you dived deep in the water to search for food. How can you do that with such small bodies?" asked Bottlenose.

Muste explained, "We have really big lungs, which allow us to store a lot of air so we can dive to the bottom of the ocean and still be able to search for food. Our lungs are probably twice as large as a land mammal of our same size."

"Tasty food is not at the surface, so we dive for it," Hydra added.

"How does the water pressure affect your bodies near the bottom of the ocean?" asked Bottlenose.

Muste explained, "Our flexible ribs allow our lungs to work properly under pressure. Also, our respiratory system allows us to deliver oxygen to our body under pressure."

"We don't like to dive too deep," yipped Hydra, "because the water pressure causes the air in our fur to escape. Then we have to spend more time grooming and replenishing the air pocket in our underfur."

"Once you're down there, how do you see under the water to find those tasty shellfish and sea urchins?" Bottlenose asked curiously.

"We have a special eye lens that lets us see in the water. We even have crystals in our eyes that help us see when the light is very low or when it is very dark," explained Hydra.

"Of course, we can smell and taste things extremely well too," chuckled Muste.

"If the ocean floor is really murky, we use our sensitive whiskers and forepaws to feel our way around to find food," Hydra said as she swam over to Bottlenose and touched her whiskers on his face.

"Well, you are just seaworthy food machines!" chattered Bottlenose.

A little embarrassed, Hydra responded, "Nah, we are just trying to survive the same as you. We don't have your speed, echolocation talent, ability to find and swallow food under the water or swimming skills. I wish we could echolocate and swim like you."

"We all have our special traits," said Bottlenose.

"I guess so," the otters replied together.

Bottlenose jumped out of the water into a double somersault. Showing off just a little, he demonstrated even more of his acrobatic talent by walking backward across the water on his tail.

"Wow, what a great water dancer!" exclaimed Hydra as both otters clapped their paws.

"Just practicing for the talent show," Bottlenose said as he beamed with pride. "I want to win the grand prize! I have to go now; my friends are echoing for me. Good luck finding your next meal." As Bottlenose leaped and twisted through the air toward his dolphin friends, he called to the otters, "See you at the talent show!"

Hydra and Muste waved goodbye to Bottlenose.

As she turned back to talk to Muste, Hydra noticed two humans in a kayak paddling toward them. "Hey, Muste, maybe those humans have some food we can eat."

"Let's be careful, Hydra. Don't forget the stories of our ancestors who swam up to the kayaks and lost their lives. The humans had fur coats and our ancestors almost disappeared from the North Pacific coastline," Muste reminded in a worried tone.

"Don't worry, Muste; the kayak has a picture of a shell. They probably come from the Nautilus Aquarium. Other otters have told me that the humans from the aquarium help sick otters and even small, orphaned otter pups." Because Hydra and Muste were curious and always looking for food, they swam closer to the kayak.

The two marine biologists—Carla and Charlie—who indeed worked at the Nautilus Aquarium, were unaware that the two otters had climbed into their boat. All of a sudden, the kayak tilted, scaring them and almost causing the boat to capsize.

A startled Carla gasped, "Oh my goodness," as Hydra plunked down in front of her. The boldness of the otters surprised Carla. Sniffing for food, Hydra inched closer to the woman.

"Carla, offer our curious otter friends a snack," said Charlie quietly. Seeing two big turban snails in the kelp, Carla plucked them out and handed them to the otters. Grinning at Carla, Hydra and Muste began to munch on the snails.

"Charlie, look at their hind feet!" exclaimed Carla in amazement.

Charlie explained, "Their outside toes are the longest and their inside toes are the smallest—just the opposite of our feet. The progressively lengthened toes help the otters swim more efficiently while they are on their backs on the surface. Under the water, they can spread their webbed feet like large swimming flippers."

"Charlie, look at those purple teeth on the female otter," chuckled Carla.

"She must really like purple sea urchins," Charlie said as he laughed. "Carla, I see two purple sea urchins eating the kelp. See if you can reach them and offer them to the otters." With their dexterous forepaws, Hydra and Muste grabbed the urchins from Carla for another tasty snack. Their sensitive, tough pads on their forepaws helped them grip the prickly sea urchins. Charlie pointed out, "Inside their paws, they have five individual fingers just like us, which help them grab their food, dig on the bottom and groom themselves. Kelp farmers like otters because they eat the sea urchins that graze on the kelp. The kelp harvested by the farmers is one of the fastest growing plants in the world. They turn it into a powder called 'alginate' that is used to thicken ice cream, yogurt and toothpaste." Then, thinking out loud, Charlie also said, "Maybe we can get the kelp farmers to donate their resources for the Nautilus otter programs." He was referring to educational programs set up to help people understand otters better.

Carla replied with excitement, "That's a perfect idea! Not only does the kelp farmer benefit from the kelp forest, but other sea creatures within the kelp too. Many marine invertebrates, such as the turban snail, crabs, fish and our otter friends, live within the kelp for a source of food, to avoid predators and to use it as a safe resting area. I'm sure these two otters prefer this kelp forest to the open sea as a 'local hangout.'"

"The otters certainly help maintain a balance in this ocean habitat," said Charlie.

"Unfortunately, increased sewage overflows, agricultural run off, pesticides, recreation vehicles, fishing equipment and rising demand to find oil in the ocean have dramatically increased environmental pressure on the otters' habitat and their rate of survival. Recent studies have revealed that the otter population has decreased in the area," Carla said in a sorrowful voice. "We, as marine biologists, must find out why the population decrease has occurred. The United States government also realized the importance of otters to the marine habitat and have passed laws protecting them."

"I understand the otters are protected under the Federal Endangered Species Act, the Marine Mammal Protection Act and the California State Mammal Protection Act," replied Charlie. "Also, this 100-mile area has been designated a sea-otter refuge, further protecting these insatiable sea-eating mammals."

Curiously, Muste and Hydra watched the biologists measure the kelp and catalog the sea creatures. Carla and Charlie hoped to learn more about the habitat of the otters and find causes for the decreasing otter population. Observing the data collection made Hydra and Muste hungry again. They decided to leave their new human friends in search of more food. As they jumped back into the water, they turned to invite Carla and Charlie, in their squeaky otter voices, to the talent show. Hydra hoped they understood, but could not resist splashing the marine biologists as she slipped back into the water.

Soaking wet, Carla turned to Charlie and said with a laugh, "I think the 'clowns of the kelp forest' were trying to tell us something, Charlie."

As Muste and Hydra reached their favorite feeding spot within the kelp forest, a huge black fin broke the water, followed quickly by another. The multiple fins looked like surfacing submarines. The otters felt their heartbeats racing. Then they realized that it was five black and white orcas—killer whales—that surrounded them.

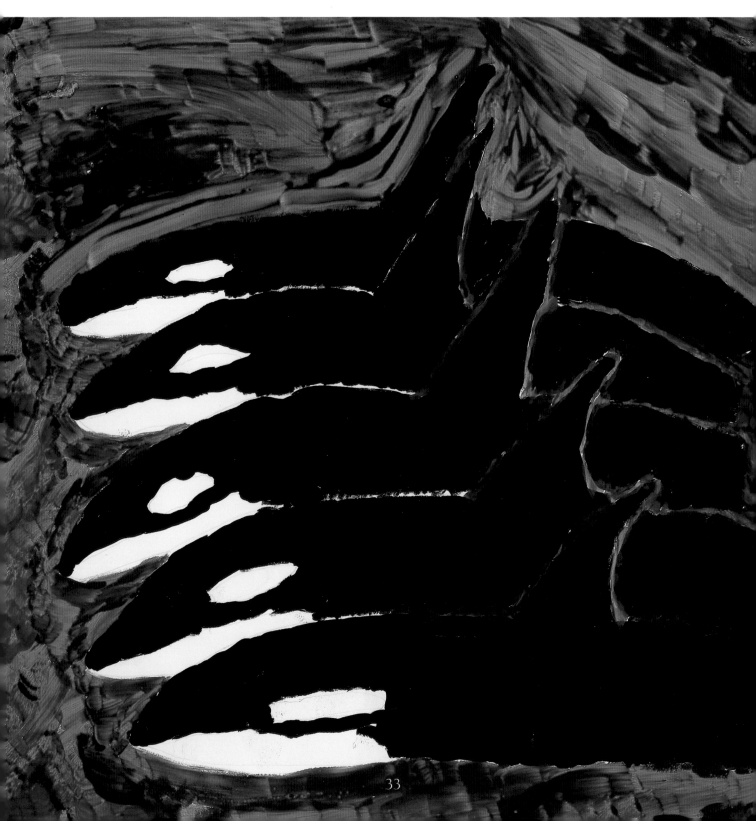

"Well, it looks like we sure surprised you," said Orcin, the leader. "We located you by our internal sonar."

"Yes, you sure startled us!" laughed Muste.

"Does your sonar send out sounds that bounce back to you like the echolocation Nova or Bottlenose use?" asked Hydra.

"Yes, you are quite smart," Orcin said as he spouted water from his blowhole. "You must have been talking to that plankton-feeding humpback whale or that chatterbox dolphin."

"Yes, we've learned about echolocation from Bottlenose," Muste revealed.

"Echolocation helps us locate tasty schools of fish," confirmed Orcin, "but we don't send out clicking sounds when we hunt for sea mammals that have their own sonar or excellent hearing. We don't want them to know we're coming so we don't lose a meal. We visually seek them out so they don't hear us." The rest of the pod huffed in agreement with Orcin.

"Wow, that's what I call stealthy hunting," yipped Muste as he took a drink of salt water.

"You can drink salt water?" questioned Orcin.

Hydra explained, "We have special kidneys that help us maintain safe levels of salt in our bodily fluids."

Muste added, "Even our favorite foods, such as invertebrates like snails and abalone, are extremely salty. Whether we drink salt water or eat salty food, our kidneys keep our bodily fluids healthy. The humans call this 'osmoregulation.'"

"Wow, I'm impressed with your knowledge of your bodies!" spouted Orcin.

"We listen to our human friends, Carla and Charlie, when they talk about us in their kayak," Hydra explained. "I'm sure you orcas have your own way to regulate salt in your bodies."

"Yes, we do," Orcin replied, unwilling to boast his knowledge in this area. Changing the subject, he asked, "By the way, did Nova have any other news?"

"He warned that Carcha might be in these waters again," Muste said.

"Have you seen Carcha lurking around here?" Hydra asked.

"No, but we'll take care of Carcha. We know how to handle *ol razor tooth*," Orcin replied in his deep voice with a sinister laugh.

"Don't worry; we won't let that bully bother you!" sputtered the others in the orca pod.

"Carcha almost had Zalo, the sea lion, for lunch, but we stopped that great white shark with a few good head butts to her side and tail whips to her head," Orcin boasted.

Another member of the pod bragged, "With the five of us there, he realized that Zalo was not going to be lunch. To thank us for saving his life, Zalo told us where we could find some elephant seals for our dinner."

"But they weren't there," the rest of the pod grumbled.

"I want to have a chat with him," said the orca leader. Swimming up close to the wide-eyed otters, Orcin spouted, "Have you seen Zalo today?"

"No, we haven't," whimpered the now trembling otters. Rapidly changing the subject, they squeaked, "Hey, Orcin, take us for a ride! If we hold on to your fin, you can take us all over the bay."

"Climb aboard," huffed Orcin. Muste and Hydra climbed on Orcin's back and took hold of his great, black dorsal fin. "Hold on! Hold on!" Orcin puffed.

Before the otters knew it, they were cruising near the bottom of the ocean with the entire orca pod. As they sped toward the surface, they swam into a school of opalescent spawning squid. With one free forepaw, both Muste and Hydra grabbed some passing squid and put them in their pouches for a later snack.

Orcin reached the surface and breached the water. The four other killer whales in the pod had followed Orcin's every move. What a sight—five orcas jumping out of the water in unison with two little otters clinging by their forepaws to Orcin's dorsal fin! The otters shrieked with delight. They loved to ride fast on the back of a killer whale; it was their favorite game. Returning the otters to their kelp forest, Orcin said goodbye. The pod had played long enough with the otters and it was time to hunt.

"Thank you for the ride," Muste said. "If we see Zalo, we'll tell him you're looking for him."

Orcin departed with a warning. "Stay close to the kelp forest when we're not around, Carcha seems to have difficulty locating prey there."

The otters shouted a reminder to Orcin about the talent show as he and his pod submerged as quickly as they had appeared. As the pod disappeared in the distance, out of the water popped Zalo, the playful sea lion.

"Hey! Are they gone? Orcin and his pod? I saw them with you from the shoreline. You can spot those black dorsal fins anywhere!" barked Zalo.

"They were looking for you," said Hydra.

"I know. I know. I didn't give them the right location of the elephant-seal hideaway. I was so upset and confused after that razor tooth, Carcha, almost had me for lunch that I gave them the wrong directions. The next time I see Orcin, I'll tell him the location of the secret elephant-seal beach. After all, he did save my life from that white terror."

"Sounds like a close call," Muste said.

"Yes, you could have been Carcha's lunch," added Hydra.

"Speaking of lunch," Zalo laughed, "I'm hungry."

Hydra and Muste pulled out the tasty squid from their storage pouches. "We'll be glad to share our squid with you," Hydra said politely, knowing the tasty snack of sun baked calamari would only be an hors d'oeuvre for the three friends.

"Hey! I found some interesting cans down by the rocks earlier. Maybe we could open them and find some food. Let's go see," barked Zalo.

"I don't know. I like my food right off the kelp," said Hydra, "not out of a can."

"Oh, Hydra!" chided Muste. "Let's go see. I watched one of my otter friends find a delicious red octopus in a can, and I know you can't resist those tasty eight-armed ink squirters!"

Muste and Hydra followed Zalo to the cans. Each can had a picture of a red skull. Not sensing the danger they were in, the otters each grabbed an end of one of the cans. They pulled and pulled. Muste's end suddenly opened and black oil gushed out. It stuck to his paws, covered his eyes and matted his fur. Muste was in trouble! The oil would destroy the protective waterproof air bubble in his underfur, which would now soak up water like a sponge. The cold water would then contact his skin and draw out body heat. Eventually Muste could die from hypothermia.

Hydra screamed at Muste, "Follow me! Follow me now! Hurry! Hurry!" Blindly, Muste followed Hydra. Hydra knew she had to get Muste out of the water. Upset that he had put his friend in danger, Zalo followed the two otters, barking encouragement to Muste. Hydra remembered that the humans at the Nautilus Aquarium helped sick or hurt otters. She guided Muste to the shore near the aquarium. By the time they reached the beach, Muste was shivering from the cold water. Hydra stopped Muste from licking the oil off his fur. She remembered hearing the marine biologists talk of the damage it can do to the kidneys, livers or digestive tracts of otters and other creatures of the sea. The memory frightened her even more and Hydra began to cry for help. It seemed as if she cried forever.

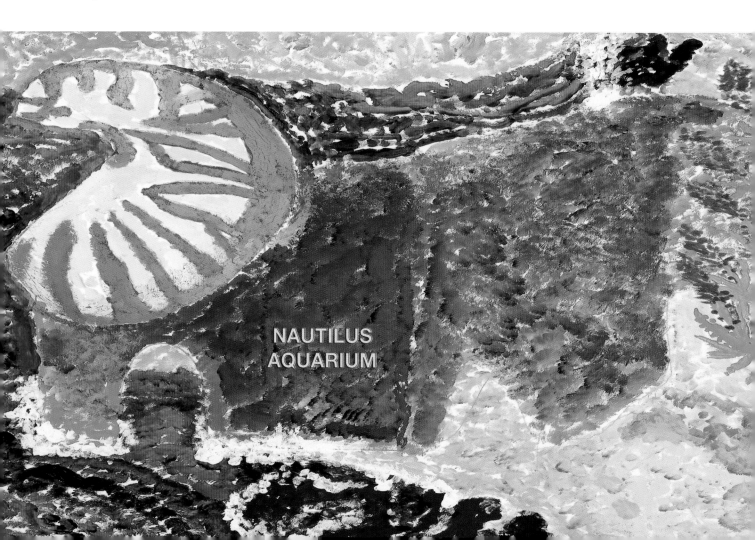

At long last, a person from the Nautilus Aquarium came to investigate the loud noises on the beach. It was Charlie, their marine biologist friend from the kayak. Realizing Muste needed help, he wrapped the oil-drenched otter in a towel and took him into the aquarium. Hydra knew Muste was in good hands, but she still felt sad and lonely as she watched him being carried away. All she could see was one limp hind foot hanging out from under the towel Charlie held in his arms.

Charlie carefully placed the shivering Muste in warm water and began washing his matted, clumped fur. He washed all of the nasty oil out of Muste's fur and helped him groom himself. Next, he put Muste under a heat lamp to warm the otter's cold body. Once Muste's body heated up, Charlie quickly took away the heat lamp and made sure the resting area was well ventilated. Otters have unusually thick fur coats and, if they have no way to cool off, can die from heat prostration.

Hydra and Zalo waited anxiously on the beach for their friend. They were so worried! Carla—the other marine biologist from the kayak—took a fish treat out to Hydra and Zalo. As she fed them, she spoke softly and tried to calm them. Zalo and Hydra were thankful for the tasty fish treat from Carla and shook her hand, but they really wanted to see Muste. They would not leave the beach. They waited and waited. As the sun dropped from the horizon, they awkwardly climbed onto some rocks with their flipperlike hind feet to rest for the night.

In the morning, a pesty osprey persistently poked Zalo and Hydra with his sharp talons. "Wake up! Wake up!" he squawked. "What are you doing here? Did you know that coyotes prowl around here looking for a tasty otter or sea lion meal? What are your names? My name is Osprey Talons. Humans sometimes call me Fish Hawk, but most creatures just call me OT."

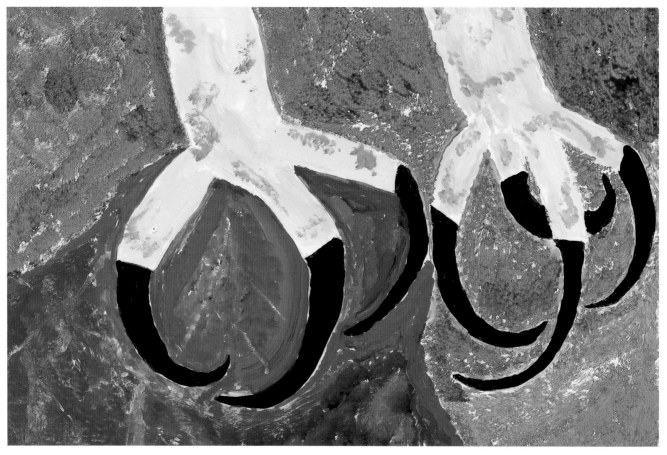

"My name is Hydra and this is Zalo, the sea lion," said Hydra in a tired voice.

"Thanks for the warning," said Zalo. "We're waiting for our otter friend, Muste. Oil coated his fur. We think the aquarium people are cleaning him up, but we haven't heard anything since last night. We are so worried about him!"

"We were so tired that we didn't even think of the hungry coyotes," squeaked Hydra. "We didn't hear any howling last night."

"I spotted a school of salmon not far away. Are you interested in eating fish this morning?" offered OT.

"I don't want to leave Muste," Hydra cried.

"Oh, we'll bring back a salmon as a treat for your friend," OT said with confidence. Zalo talked Hydra into following OT, who flew over their heads leading them to the fish.

Suddenly, OT flew closer and closer to the surface of the water and, with his talons extended forward, hooked a salmon without even getting wet. After catching fish for the three of them, OT looked for one more fish to bring back for Muste. This time, he splashed into the water, wings and water flying in all directions. After what seemed like a very long time to the astonished onlookers, OT finally surfaced with a large salmon. He turned the head of the fish forward to reduce wind resistance and flew back to a very impressed Hydra and Zalo.

Zalo whispered to Hydra, "Now I know why OT is called a fish hawk."

With full tummies, all three returned to the aquarium beach. On the shore, there stood Charlie and Carla with Muste at their side, patiently waiting for Hydra and Zalo to return. Hydra jumped with excitement when she saw Muste alive and the oil off his fur. Muste squeaked his gratitude to his aquarium friends for saving his life. Climbing into their kayak, Charlie and Carla motioned to the otters to lead them to the cans of oil. Muste and Hydra understood what the humans wanted, and with Zalo and OT tagging along, led them to the location of the oil cans. Spotting the oil slick on the water, Charlie and Carla radioed the Coast Guard for help to get the messy oil cleaned up. Muste warned the others to keep their distance from the cans. With Zalo swimming alongside, Muste and Hydra squeaked their thanks once again to the humans and swam away.

Flying overhead, the keen-eyed OT noticed a dark shape on the ocean floor. "Hey, I think I've found a sunken ship," he squawked.

Muste and Hydra were very curious. Zalo said he felt uneasy about exploring a sunken ship. He knew that sharks liked to hang around old sunken ships just waiting for creatures to come exploring.

"I'll keep an eye out," OT screeched.

As OT hovered above, the trio cautiously dived toward the ship. They saw a mast rising through the fronds of kelp. The sun filtered through the kelp fronds, giving the ship an eerie green image.

Red sea anemones and orange cup coral grew everywhere.

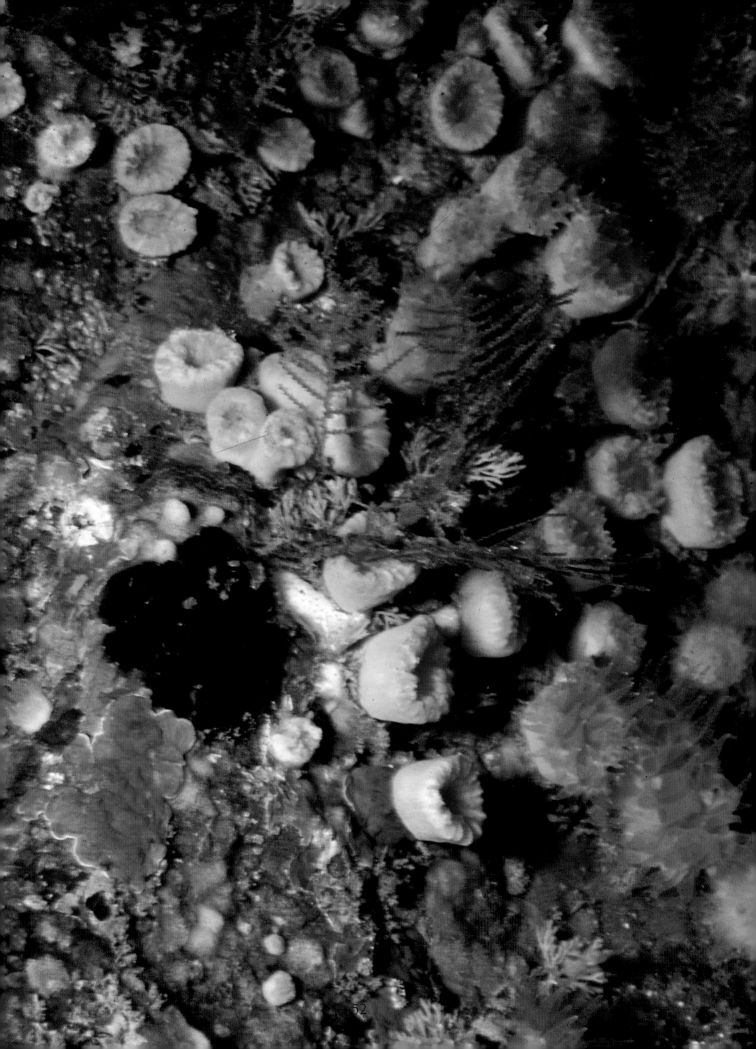

Hydra wanted to look inside to see if there were any little red octopuses that were so good to eat. Muste and Zalo were nervous, but they followed the bold little Hydra inside the gloomy ship. Zalo kept looking for shadows through the portholes. The three explorers found big black balls and long metal tubes on the deck of the sunken ship. They looked in the tubes for food and playfully rolled the big black balls down the deck. As one ball broke through the floor of the deck, horror struck them. A skull floated up from the deck below. The three nearly jumped out of their skins as they rushed to the surface.

Once on the surface and safe, they laughed at how silly they had acted. After all, an old skull could not hurt them.

Zalo said, "On our way up to the surface, I noticed your ears back and now they are up. Why is that?" he asked.

"Moving our ears back creates a water barrier when we swim underwater," Hydra explained. "On the surface, we don't hold them back so we can hear better." Hydra felt brave again. "Let's go back down and see what else we can find," she yipped.

"What did you find the first time?" squawked OT from above.

"Nothing tasty yet," Hydra answered, and with that, back down they went.

As OT continued to circle above them, the trio swam deep inside the ship, moving old tools out of their way. Inside one small compartment, they found shiny red and green rocks and round silver and gold pieces of metal that reflected the rays of the sun that filtered down from the surface of the water. As beautiful as the colored rocks were, they knew they couldn't eat them and continued their search for food.

Seemingly out of nowhere, a dark shadow moved slowly across the ship. Zalo began to shiver.

"Could that be Carcha?" he asked aloud. The brave explorers lost much of their courage as they huddled together and kept very still. Suddenly, the ship rocked violently — then again and again. Their greatest fear had come true; it was Carcha.

The great white shark rammed the ship with her head once more, trying to scare the three out. OT had seen the huge fin of the shark earlier on the surface from his bird's eye view. He knew he had to get Carcha's attention for the others to escape the ship. He also knew they must be desperate for air by now. OT courageously dived from the air, broke the surface of the water and came within inches of Carcha. Success! The great white shark turned and chased OT. OT broke the surface and began running on the water, flapping his wet wings as he tried desperately to take flight. Carcha opened her massive jaws and just missed OT's talons as the terrified osprey lifted toward the sky.

The three terrified explorers scooted out of the ship and rapidly swam for shore. They could feel the hungry beast speeding toward them now! Just as they jumped out of the water onto the rocks, Carcha's huge dorsal fin surfaced. Her razor-sharp teeth lunged at Zalo. With her mouth wide open, Carcha just missed the sea lion's tail as Zalo jumped safely onto the rocks. The shark was so close, all three of them could clearly see the rage in her piercing black eyes as she splashed them with her tail and swam away.

"Yes, she missed her tasty meal," squeaked Muste in a nervous voice.

"She was definitely having one of her shark tantrums," barked Zalo.

"I'm just glad we're all alive," sighed Hydra. "We really appreciate your bravery, OT."

"Thanks for saving our lives," cheered the trio.

Embarrassed, OT replied, "Well, it was my idea to explore the ship. I felt responsible for you so I had to do something."

Jokingly, Zalo announced, "Let's not invite Carcha to the talent show."

After their dramatic experience with white death, the three explorers curled up together and fell asleep on the rocks. Perching on the higher rocks above them, OT watched for coyotes with one eye open while his comrades fell asleep and recovered from what could have been a fatal encounter.

All of them awoke hungry. Muste and Hydra found some abalone and clams to eat. Zalo caught a fat salmon that he shared with OT. As they enjoyed their tasty feast, they laughed and sang, "It's great to be alive! It's great to be alive!"

"So what do you want to do today?" OT squawked eagerly.

"Today's the talent show," Muste grinned.

"Yes, today is the day!" exclaimed Hydra with excitement.

Knowing he had some explaining to do, Zalo hesitated. Hydra said gently, "They're going to find you eventually, Zalo. You might as well come with us and face them." Reluctantly, Zalo tagged along with Hydra and Muste as OT followed above them. When they reached the beach, the area for the talent show was unusually quiet. Hydra wondered if they had the right date and time. She called to OT, "Do you see anyone?"

"I see Biros, the giant manta ray, near the shore," OT reported.

"Who is the master of ceremonies for this talent show?" asked Zalo.

"I think Biros is announcing the show," replied Muste.

All of a sudden the beach and water were alive with activity. Bottlenose breached the water, creating a large splash near Hydra, Muste and Zalo. He flipped in the air and danced on his tail. "Am I late for the show?" he chattered.

Then Nova breached the water, too. Delphi and her common dolphin friends twisted high out of the water. On the beach, Phoca, the harbor seal, balanced a ball on her nose. Of course, OT had to get into the act. He spun, twisted and leveled off just above the water as he grabbed a fish with his talons without getting a drop of water on him or missing a beat of his wings.

To start the talent show, Biros blew a fanfare on a large conch shell and announced the judges. As he introduced Triak as the first judge, the leopard shark swam through the kelp. To acknowledge her position as the second judge, Dali, the Dall's porpoise performed a magnificent flip high in the air. Bala, the blue whale, waved his hug pectoral flipper at the crowd in response to being introduced as the third judge.

And what an audience there was for the talent show this year! Whales, dolphins, sea otters, rockfish, sharks, bat rays and dogfish were all now arriving to enjoy the entertainment and see their friends compete. Even the pelicans, great egrets and blue herons, perched in the bleacher section, squawked their excitement. Carla and Charlie from the Nautilus Aquarium were there to cheer on all the participants from the sea.

When Biros introduced the first performer, Nova breached the water, exposing his entire body before hitting the surface in a titanic splash. Then, as he demonstrated his famous whale-tail-sail, he flipped Hydra and Muste through the air and finished with his favorite song. The crowd loved his act!

Next, Delphi and her two common dolphin friends synchronized amazing jumps in the air. Their act looked like a polished water ballet. Over and over they jumped together. They must have really practiced. The crowd responded with loud applause for the dolphins.

OT performed his high-flying acrobatics, finishing with a large salmon hooked to his sharp talons. The crowd cheered and cheered for the talented flying osprey.

Biros then introduced Bottlenose, who began with his tail walk and a high jumping somersault. He completed his act with a tremendous double somersault. The crowd roared its approval of his acrobatic water skills.

Zalo and Phoca balanced balls on their noses. Then Zalo balanced Phoca on his nose. What an impressive act by the barking sea lion and harbor seal! The crowd applauded loudly.

Biros waited for the audience to quiet before announcing the next act. At that moment, five huge black fins emerged from the water. Orcin and his pod performed their spectacular simultaneous breaches. The five majestic black and white mammals dazzled the crowd. The act ended with Hydra and Muste hanging onto Orcin's dorsal fin as he leaped high out of the water in a triumphant, final breach. The crowd loved watching the otters join the orca pod's act.

The judges voted first place to the orca pod. Every sea creature cheered! Orcin was very proud of his pod. Just as Biros was going to present the first-place prize, a big gray dorsal fin sliced through the water, heading directly for Delphi and the other dolphins. Bottlenose rapidly clicked a warning to them! At the last moment, the dolphins moved out of the way, just as Carcha's big jaws snapped shut next to Delphi, collecting only water.

Disgusted by the shark's intrusion, Orcin and his pod decided to teach Carcha a lesson. The killer whales each smacked Carcha with their tails. They even butted the nasty shark with their noses. One of the killer whales breached the water and crashed on top of the great white shark. Battered and bruised, Carcha swam away.

"Three cheers for the orca pod!" yelled the crowd.

"That should teach that sneaky set of jaws not to hunt our friends and then join our fun uninvited," huffed Orcin. He was so proud of his pod that he forgot all about Zalo's little folly and the wild-goose chase to find elephant seals. Biros awarded the orca pod their blue ribbons and their first-place prize of a year's supply of herring. The pod decided to share some of the prize with Nova, who just loved herring.

Muste, Hydra and their friends had a great time at the talent show. "What a wonderful, wonderful day," Hydra said to Muste as they swam slowly back to their favorite kelp forest near the slough. Wrapping themselves in kelp, they fell asleep dreaming of adventures yet to be.

Then, seemingly out of nowhere, the surface rippled as a dark shadow moved slowly across the rocks below the surface. . . .

George Kingston, Author

A graduate from California State University, Chico, with a degree in biology, George Kingston also received an MBA from San Francisco State University. In addition to an accomplished author, George serves as a certified financial planner and financial advisor. Success as a financial advisor has allowed him to follow his heart, which often leads him to adventures of the sea. His lifelong interest in nature and the marine world is manifested in this book, which provided an invaluable opportunity to further research the sea world through the lives of otters. The project also enabled George to offer children an endearing tale to spark their own interest in the magnificent animals of the sea and nature in general. George continues to live and work in Los Gatos, California, approximately 20 miles from Santa Cruz. His first book, *Goldilocks Makes Friends*, began his own personal adventure as a unique storyteller for children across the globe.

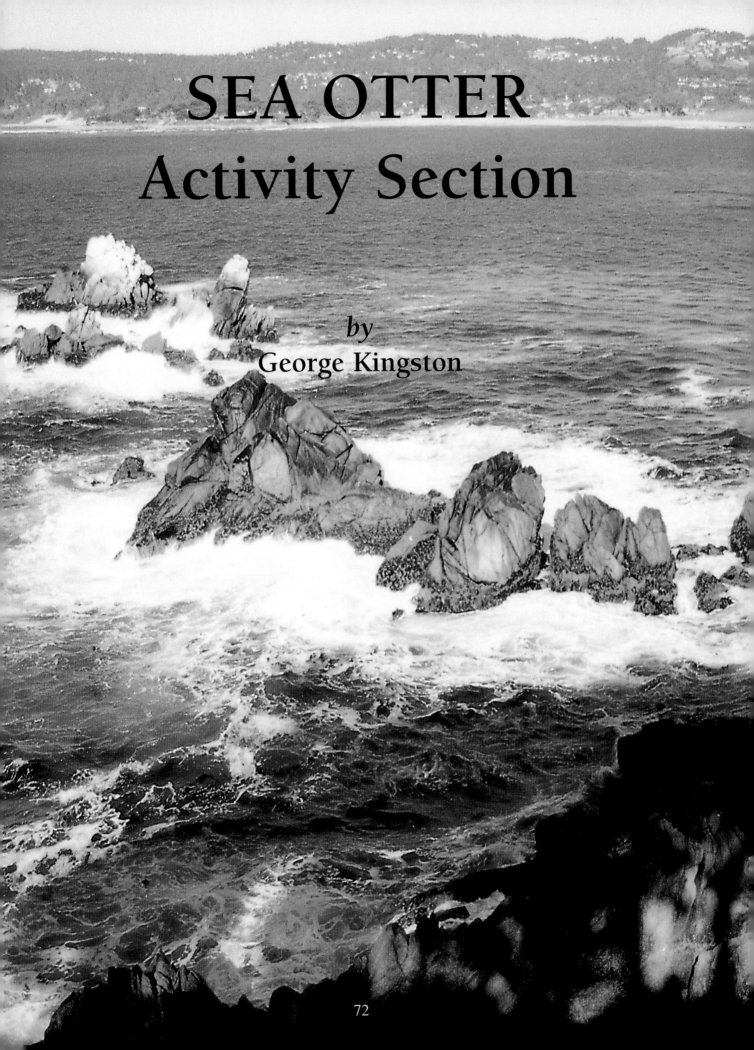

SEA OTTER
Activity Section

by
George Kingston

CONTENTS

FIND HIDDEN WORDS 74

CROSSWORD PUZZLE 75

WHAT AM I 77

WORD SCRAMBLE 79

OT'S DETECTIVE ACTIVITY 80

MEMORY FUN 81

CRYPTIC MESSAGE OF THE KELP FOREST 88

CREATE WORDS 89

MAZE 90

GLOSSARY 91

ANIMAL AND PLANT CLASSIFICATION 96

ANSWER KEY 98

CONTRIBUTORS TO STORY 102

PHOTOGRAPH AND ILLUSTRATION CREDITS 103

FIND THE HIDDEN WORDS

Nova wants to see if you can find the words from the story that are hidden in the box below. Look for the words either across or down. Words can be spelled either forwards or backwards.

```
A J V A L S P Q A L P B P O C T O P U S U D
B O X E J U H O C O N D N U E D S Q G U Y T
S E A O T T E R W N O T K N A L P P I B V G
L K B B P W F R E M S H R T F M R R K M C M
O N A L G I N A T E Q C F A H R E N H E I T
U P L D K T L P G C U E O W K S Y Z M R B J
G R O O M X I V B H A B I T A T S A L G X F
H L N Z N V E T X O X I Q D Y H T L A E T S
G R E N I R A M D L R O R C A N T B J O Z K
F Q W C M B J A I O W L F V K E L P M S M N
I M Y F R A F T F C T F L C H G U F A Q O P
D I T N O Y M T K A Y J U X G U W H M T R L
H F A N F A R E Y T V G K Z J F Y C M P S E
G T L H Q C G D H I N V E R T E B R A T E S
P R O W L A K S P O D M S Y A R U E L U L H
E U N G R Z N U Z N A K S B I O X D N R A O
```

ABALONE	HABITAT
ALGINATE	INVERTEBRATES
ECHOLOCATION	KAYAK
FANFARE	KELP
FAHRENHEIT	MAMMAL
FLUKES	MARINE
GROOM	MATTED
MORSEL	RAFT
OCTOPUS	REFUGE
ORCA	SEA OTTER
OSPREY	SLOUGH
PLANKTON	STEALTHY
POD	SUBMERGE
PROWL	TALON

CROSSWORD PUZZLE

Muste had fun creating this puzzle for you.
Use his clues on the next page and complete each crossword.

75

ACROSS:
2. An edible sea mollusk with an oval shell
5. To make calm
7. Ability to bend without breaking
11. A boat with a small opening for the paddler
13. A kelp stipe and attached blades
15. Clicking signals that determine distance, position, and size of an object under the water
17. An iridescent silica of various colors
20. Of or found in the sea
21. The use of sound waves to find objects in the water
22. Small bite or portion of food
23. Free-swimming shrimplike crustaceans
25. An appetizer served before a meal
26. Complex pattern of grunts, squeals, or whistles of a humpback whale
28. To place or sink beneath the surface of the water
29. Extremely chilling condition, which may be life threatening
32. Thick tangle
34. To roll, touch, and clean otter fur
35. Two or more sea otters together
36. Physical and chemical changes within a living organism
40. Nostril(s) used for breathing on the top of the head of a whale
41. Sea mammal with dense hair that loves to eat sea invertebrates (two words)
42. Shelter or protection from danger or difficulty
44. Narrow salt or fresh waterway edged with muddy and marshy ground
46. Inner fur layer of an otter
47. Organs that secrete hormones, enzymes, water, or oil
49. Performing the same action at the same time
50. The claw of a bird of prey
51. Victorious
52. To move slowly in a winding course
53. Process of controlling heat within the body
54. Sea mollusk with eight arms and two long tentacles

DOWN:
1. Unit for measuring the energy produced by food
2. Derived from kelp and used as a thickener
3. High-frequency sounds produced by echolocating sea mammals
4. Two horizontal, flattened divisions in the tail of a whale
6. To move to another region with the change in seasons
8. To leap out of the water
9. To eat greedily or hungrily
10. Thankful appreciation
12. Large, brown seaweed
14. Large fin located along the midline of the back of a whale
16. A mollusk with eight arms covered with suckers
18. Front cutting tooth
19. Outer fur layer of an otter (two words)
24. Animals that lack a spinal column and internal skeleton
25. Environment of a plant or animal
27. Warm-blooded sea animal with hair that nurses its young and breathes air
30. Another name for a killer whale
31. Loud flourish of trumpets; noisy or showy display
33. Process of maintaining constant salinity in the body
37. A large hawklike bird that mainly feeds on fish
38. Feeding strategy used by humpback whales to confuse herring (two words)
39. Secretly acting or moving undercover
43. Something that blocks or hinders
45. Cooked squid
48. Long-term social group of orca whales

WHAT AM I?

Carcha snaps, " Using the clues below, guess the creatures in the story."

1. I have a gray or brown upper body surface with white underneath and elongated body, which may grow to twenty feet. My snout is pointed. I feed on large fish, sea otters, seals, sea lions and elephant seals with my triangular and serrate teeth in coastal waters.

   _ _ _ _ _   _ _ _ _ _   _ _ _ _ _

2. I am slender with a dark blue upper body, bright blue on my sides and white underneath. My snout is long and narrowly rounded. I feed on small schooling fish and squid with my serrated teeth.

   _ _ _ _   _ _ _ _ _

3. I am gray with black spots and bars, which may stretch across my back. My snout is moderately long and pointed. I feed on fish, crustaceans, crabs and shrimp in shallow bays.

   _ _ _ _ _ _ _   _ _ _ _ _

4. I have a large gray body that could grow to fifty feet or more, with very large pectoral fins. I love to eat krill and herring. I enjoy vocalizing songs during my seasonal migration to Alaska.

   _ _ _ _ _ _ _   _ _ _ _ _

5. I can grow to twelve feet with shades of gray. I like to jump high out of the water and feed on fish, squid, shrimp and crabs. I have echolocation powers.

   _ _ _ _ _ _ _ _ _   _ _ _ _ _ _

6. I can grow to thirty feet with black and white markings on my body. My dorsal fin is quite large. I love to eat elephant seals, fish, squid, sea turtles, sea birds and other edible animals in the sea. I am social and travel in pods.

_ _ _ _ _ _   _ _ _ _ _

7. I live in cool coastal waters, which have plenty of nutrients. My body parts consist of a stipe, holdfast, and blades. I can produce my own food and grow up to 100 feet. I need a hard surface for attachment.

_ _ _ _ _   _ _ _ _ _

8. I am slender and about four feet long. I live in the ocean and like to stay in the kelp. I have the densest fur of all animals in the world. I love to eat invertebrates such as clams, sea urchins and abalone.

_ _ _ _   _ _ _ _ _ _

9. I am slender with a brown body. I love to eat fish and can swim fast. I have long front flippers and prominent ears.

_ _ _ _   _ _ _ _ _

10. I love to hunt for fish by diving into the water. I have a brownish and white coloring with a darkish band across my eyes.

_ _ _ _ _ _

11. I can reach twenty-two feet in width. I am blackish above and pale below mixed with dark blotches. My pectoral fins are wing-like. I seem to fly through the water.

_ _ _ _ _   _ _ _ _ _ _   _ _ _

WORD SCRAMBLE

Zalo says, "The words from our story are all scrambled below. Unscramble each word and place it in the blanks. Then place each letter above the corresponding numbered blank at the bottom to find the message about sharks. If the number repeats at the bottom, repeat the same corresponding letter."

1. TEORT _ _ _ _ _
             6 4

2. REBAHC _ _ _ _ _ _
          12   3 13

3. KLFSUE _ _ _ _ _ _
          10 7   5 6

4. AHBTTIA _ _ _ _ _ _ _
          2   9   14

5. AAKKY _ _ _ _ _
          3 15 3

6. BLAOANE _ _ _ _ _ _ _
          3   7 11 6

7. ACRO _ _ _ _
          3

8. SPYERO _ _ _ _ _ _
          1 8   6

9. LSUGOH _ _ _ _ _ _
          1 7   2

10. SDIUQ _ _ _ _ _
          1   9

Find the Message:

_ _ _ _ _ _ _ _ _ _ _ _ _
1 2 3 4 5 1 2 6 7 8 1 6 3

_ _ _ _ _ _ _ _ _ _ _ _ _ _ _ _
7 9 10 6 1 14 3 15 9 11 12 3 7 3 11 13 6

OT'S DETECTIVE ACTIVITY

From the clues below, determine which food each character prefers to eat. For this activity, each animal will prefer only one type of food.

Muste and Hydra prefer to eat invertebrates.

Nova, Bottlenose, OT and Zalo prefer to eat fish.

Nova likes to eat fish that become confused by bubbles.

Clams and sea urchins are invertebrates.

Salmon like to swim in cold water.

Sea urchins love to eat kelp.

Orcin and Carcha prefer to eat sea mammals.

Carcha likes to eat the sea mammal with the most blubber.

Bottlenose prefers to eat the smallest fish in alphabetical order.

Sardines are larger than anchovies but smaller than herring, which is the not the largest fish.

Osprey Talons prefers to eat the largest fish.

Bubbles confuse herring.

Elephant seals have more blubber than harbor seals, which are both sea mammals.

Hydra prefers to eat animals that eat kelp.

Tip: List the characters down and the type of food across on a chart. Put an "O" for a false answer and an "X" a true answer.

Memory Fun

Orcin wonders how much you remember about the story. Try and answer the questions he has and test your logic and riddle skills too. Each question may have more than one answer.

1. What did Hydra eat?

    a) sea urchins   b) crabs   c) clams   d) turban snails   e) abalone

2. What did Muste eat?

    a) sea urchins   b) clams   c) crabs   d) abalone   e) turban snails

3. Is it important that otters prefer different food?

    Yes / No (circle one)

4. Why does a kelp forest make a great habitat for the sea otter?

    a) food
    b) reduced drifting from tides and currents
    c) protection from rough seas
    d) protection from predators
    e) learn to tie kelp knots

5. How did Hydra open her clams?

    a) teeth   b) rock   c) a second clam   d) did not open clams

6. How did Hydra use a rock during feeding?

    a) hit the food on a rock
    b) used the rock to hit the food
    c) did not use a rock

7. How did Muste use a rock during feeding?

    a) hit the food on a rock
    b) used the rock to hit the food
    c) did not use a rock

8. Number the following characters in the order in which they appeared in the story:

    ___Carcha   ___Nova   ___Bottlenose   ___OT

    ___Orcin   ___Charlie and Carla   ___Zalo

9. Why do otters keep their paws and flippers out of the water?

    a) reduced amount of fur on both paws and flippers
    b) sun's rays warm paws and flippers
    c) like to play "paddy cake"
    d) both a and b

10. Why do otters wrap themselves in kelp?

    a) keep them from floating away because of tides
    b) keep them from floating away because of currents
    c) like to stay near the raft
    d) all of the above

11. How do otters stay warm?

    a) blubber
    b) dense fur
    c) hot-water bottle
    d) King Neptune's tanning salon

12. Otters are the only marine mammal without a layer of fat.

    True / False (circle one)

13. The dense otter fur consists of guard hairs and underfur.

    True / False (circle one)

14. Assign the letter with the correct definition to each of the following words from the story:

    ___hypothermia   ___thermoregulation   ___metabolism

    ___echolocation   ___osmoregulation

    a. loss of body heat; can result in death
    b. clicking sounds used to determine position, size, and distance of objects under the water
    c. constant body temperature
    d. maintains proper salt balance in bodily fluids
    e. rate at which body burns food calories

15. Approximately what percentage of their body weight do otters eat every day?

    a) 25%   b) 33%   c) 50%   d) a or b

16. Why do otters roll and touch each other?

    a) help trap air bubbles between hairs to form protective pocket of air
    b) increase skin circulation
    c) spread natural oils on skin and fur
    d) fun

17. An otter can touch every part of its body.

    True / False (circle one)

18. Why do otters groom themselves?

    a) keep fur from getting matted
    b) maintain air pocket in underfur so cold water will not touch skin surface
    c) personal hygiene
    d) none of the above

19. Can you name three ways an otter grooms itself?

    a) _____

    b) _____

    c) _____

20. What kind of sea life does Nova like to eat?

    a) krill   b) herring   c) plankton   d) otters

21. A raft consists of five or more otters.

    True / False (circle one)

22. Match the following humpback-whale parts to the correct location in the diagram on the next page by noting the proper letter.

    ___dorsal fin   ___flukes   ___pectoral fin   ___blow hole   ___tubercles

23. What do great-white sharks like to eat?

    a) elephant seals   b) sea lions   c) dolphins   d) harbor seals

24. An otter can dive over 60 feet under the water.

    True / False (circle one)

25. An otter cannot see under the water.

    True / False (circle one)

26. When the ocean bottom is murky, how does an otter search for food?

    a) uses whiskers
    b) feels with paws
    c) flashlight
    d) uses light from luminescent fish

27. Do otters eat food under the water?

    Yes / No (circle one)

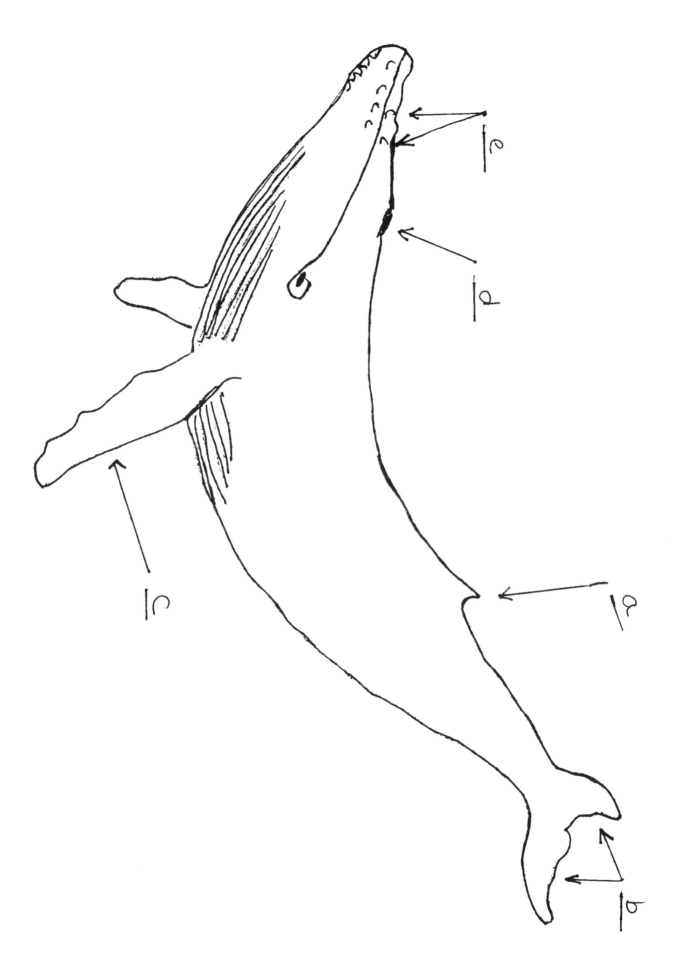

28. Place the correct letter from the list below next to the appropriate story characters.

    a) great water dancer   ___Bottlenose

    b) countershaded body   ___Carcha

    c) protected Zalo from Carcha   ___Nova

    d) whale-tail-sail   ___Muste

    e) spotted sunken ship   ___Zalo

    f) knew the secret elephant-seal hideaway ___Orcin

    g) lives in the kelp   ___OT

29. What kind of shell is painted on the marine-biologists kayak?

    a) clam   b) crab   c) nautilus   d) mussel

30. The outer toes of otters are longer than their inner toes, while humans have inner toes longer than their outer toes.

    True / False (circle one)

31. Which character in the story had purple teeth after eating?

    a) Hydra   b) Muste   c) Carcha   d) Orcin

32. Who (1) likes or (2) dislikes sea otters? Place one of the two numbers next to each:

    a) sea invertebrates___   b) kelp farmers___   c) Nautilus aquarium___   d) you, the reader ___

33. What environmental factors have put pressure on the otter habitat?

    a) increased sewage overflows
    b) agricultural runoff
    c) pesticides
    d) recreational vehicles
    e) fishing equipment

34. What were the marine biologists studying in the ocean when they came upon Muste and Hydra?

    a) the decline of the otter population
    b) the different types of sea creatures in the ocean
    c) the location of the otters' local "hangout"
    d) the sea-otter habitat

35. What law(s) have been enacted to protect the otter?

    a) Federal Endangered Species Act
    b) Marine Mammal Protection Act
    c) California State Mammal Protection Act
    d) Designated sea otter refuge

36. Sonar is to sound as echolocation is to _____.

    a) whale songs   b) clicks   c) radio waves   d) eye sight

37. Orcin is to killer whales as Nova is to _____.

    a) stars   b) mammals   c) humpback whales   d) blowholes

38. Carcha is to seal lions as Muste is to _____.

    a) abalone   b) dolphins   c) Hydra   d) kelp

39. Killer whales generally use echolocation to hunt other echolocating sea mammals.

    True / False (circle one)

40. While riding on Orcin, the otters grabbed _____.

    a) sea urchins
    b) kelp
    c) turban snails
    d) opalescent spawning squid

41. Match the sound with the animal:

    bark___   bellow___   eek___   squawk___   squeak___   spouted___

    a) Bottlenose   b) Zalo   c) Nova   d) Hydra/Muste   e) OT   f) Orcin

42. Squid is to calamari as clams are to _____.

    a) oysters   b) steamed clams   c) mollusks   d) shells

43. You eat an hors d'oeuvre _____ dinner.

    a) after   b) before

44. Place the correct letter from the list below next to the appropriate story characters:

    Carcha___   OT___   red octopus___   Nova___   Muste/Hydra___   Bottlenose___

    a) eight-armed ink squirter   b) razor tooth   c) fish hawk   d) song composer

    e) clowns of the kelp forest   f) chatterbox

45. A picture of a red skull on a container represents possible danger.

    True / False (circle one)

46. How does oil affect an otter?

    a) mats the fur and destroys the protective waterproof air bubble
    b) damages the kidneys and/or liver if licked
    c) allows cold water to contact otter skin
    d) all of the above

47. Otters cannot overheat.

    True / False (circle one)

48. The osprey in the story was known as _____.

    a) Osprey Talons   b) OT   c) fish hawk   d) fish breath

49. What animal(s) almost felt the jaws of Carcha?

    a) OT   b) Zalo   c) Delphi   d) Bottlenose   e) Orcin

50. Otter ears are _____ when under the water.

    a) forward   b) back

51. Match the animal activity in the talent show to the correct story character:

    a) whale-tail-sail   ___OT

    b) synchronized jumps   ___Nova

    c) high-flying acrobatics   ___Zalo

    d) somersault   ___Bottlenose

    e) balance ball   ___Orcin and pod

    f) simultaneous breaches   ___Delphi and friends

52. Place the correct letter from the below list related to the talent show next to the appropriate story characters:

    a) won first prize   ___Triak

    b) served as a judge   ___Orcin and pod

    c) kept an eye out for coyotes on the beach   ___blue heron

    d) served as a master of ceremonies   ___OT

    e) spectator   ___Biros

    f) used for fanfare   ___Carcha

    g) an uninvited guest   ___Conch

53. What do otters and Tom Sawyer have in common?

54. What did the female otter say to the male otter before they were married?

Cryptic Message
Of The Kelp Forest

Hydra found a tablet on the ocean floor. The otters are curious about the ancient writing. Please use the cryptic symbol key to decipher the massage.

Cryptic Message Key

LETTER	SYMBOL	LETTER	SYMBOL
A	α	B	β
C	X	D	Δ
E	э	F	Φ
G	Γ	H	σ
I	∞	J	ϑ
K	∇	L	Λ
M	∅	N	&
O	φ	P	Π
Q	Θ	R	λ
S	Σ	T	⊗
U	∩	V	ς
W	Ω	X	Ξ
Y	Ψ	Z	∝

Σэα φ⊗⊗эλΣ σэΛΠ Πλφ⊗эX⊗

⊗σэ ∇эΛΠ ΦφλэΣ⊗ βΨ эα⊗∞&Γ

⊗σэ Σэα ∞&ςэλ⊗эβλα⊗эΣ

⊗σα⊗ ΦээΔ φ& ⊗σэ ∇эΛΠ.

CREATE WORDS

Carla and Charlie ask, "How many English words can you find hidden within Muste and Hydra's family name, "MUSTELIDAE"? We know there are over 100 words. Can you find 50 of them?

UNDERWATER CAVE

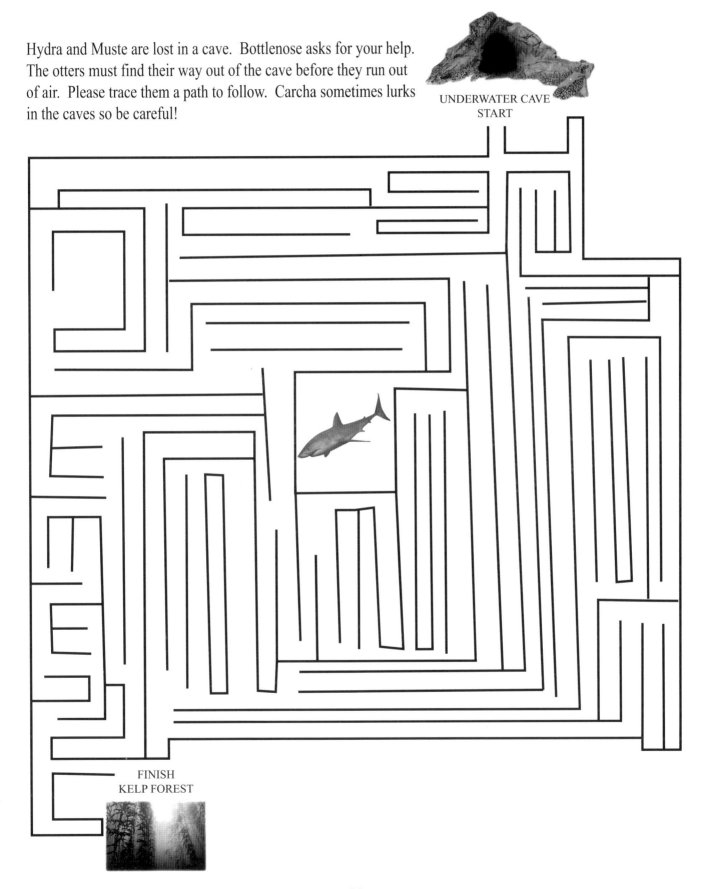

GLOSSARY

Abalone — An edible sea mollusk with a pearlescent shell in a rough oval shape.

Alginate, Algin — A carbohydrate extracted from brown marine algae, widely used for its water-binding, thickening and emulsifying properties.

Baleen — The comblike fibrous plates hanging from the upper jaw that are used to filter food from sea water, often referred to as *whalebone* in some whales.

Barrier — Anything that blocks or hinders.

Bellow — To utter loudly or powerfully, to roar with a reverberating sound.

Blowhole — Nostril(s) located on top of the heads of whales to breath air. During dives, the blowhole is sealed by a nasal plug, which is retracted by fast-acting muscles upon reaching the surface for breathing. Baleen whales have two blowholes; toothed whales have one.

Breach — To leap out of the water and landing back with a loud splash.

Bubble net feeding — A form of hunting used by humpback whales that produces a net of bubbles causing prey to cluster tightly so more can be caught easily.

Calamari — Cooked squid.

Calorie — A unit for measuring the energy produced by food once oxidized in the body.

Chide — To rebuke, express disapproval or reprove mildly.

Circulation — Movement in a circle or specified circuit and return, such as movement of blood through the arteries and veins.

Clicking — A series of close-spaced broad-spectrum sounds, mainly at high frequencies, produced by animals that echolocate. Each species has distinct frequencies and patterns of clicks.

Coast Guard — A governmental force employed to defend the coasts of our nation, aid vessels in distress and monitor pollution cleanup.

Compose — To put into proper form, to make calm.

Countershading — Protective coloring of some marine species in which the animals are darker on the upper dorsal surface than on their lower ventral surface, causing them to appear evenly colored and inconspicuous whether seen from above or below.

Crustacea — A class of arthropod animals, such as lobsters and crabs, with jointed feet and mandibles; two pairs of antennae; and segmented, chitin-cased bodies.

Devour — To eat hungrily, to consume greedily.

Dorsal fin — Large fin located along the midline of the backs of most fish and cetaceans.

Echolocation	A process of using echoes (sounds reflecting off distant objects) to locate objects such as prey; the detection of an object by means of reflected sound. The animal emits a sound, usually at a very high frequency, which bounces off another object and returns as an echo. Interpreting the echo and the time required for its return allows the animal to determine the position, distance and size of the object, helping it to navigate and find food.
Endotherm	*Endo* means within and *therm* refers to heat. Our bodies are kept warm by the large amount of body heat produced by working cells and muscle tissue. Whales, seals, dolphins and marine birds have a metabolic rate that generates body heat that is retained by body insulation such as blubber and feathers. This enables these animals to conserve costly energy and increase internally generated heat and endurance.
Fahrenheit	Points of measure on a thermometer (32 degrees Fahrenheit = freezing point; 212 degrees Fahrenheit = the boiling point of water).
Fanfare	A loud flourish of trumpets; noisy or showy display.
Filter feeding	Small schooling fish and zooplankton suspended in seawater become trapped inside the mouth cavity, which is then forced through the matted, bristles of the baleen plates filtering the food for the cetacean.
Flexibility	Ability to bend without breaking; pliability.
Flukes	One of the two horizontally flattened divisions of the tail of a whale. In cetaceans, the horizontally flattened tail fin.
Frond	A kelp stipe (the stalk portion) and the attached blades (the leafy portion).
Glands	Organs that secrete substances for the body to use or discard.
Gratitude	Thankful appreciation for favors received.
Groom	To make neat and tidy.
Guard hairs	Outer fur layer of an otter.
Habitat	Place where a plant or animal lives, a home. The type of environment in which a species is found naturally and that provides the biological and physical conditions the species requires to sustain life.
Heat prostration	Overcome by heat.
Holdfast	The part of seaweed that holds the plant to a firm surface known as a *substrate* by rootlike branches called *haptera*.
Hors d'oeuvre	An appetizer served before a meal.
Hypothermia	Life-threatening, extreme chilling.
Incisor	Any of the front cutting teeth between the canine teeth.
Kayak	A type of canoe with a small opening for the paddler.

Kelp	Any of the large brown seaweed such as Macrocystis (giant kelp). Golden-green Macrocystis pyrifera—flat-bladed giant kelp—grow to 100 feet. Single-stalked bull kelp—Nereocystis luetkeana—grow what is known as a *bullwhip crown* of blades buoyed up by one round float. Kelp belongs to the plant group called *algae*. Brown, green, and red algae prefer to attach to rocks on the ocean bottom. Kelp needs waterborne nutrients and sunlight.
Krill	Shrimplike crustaceans—Genus euphausia—live in large populations within certain seas and are the principal food of some whales and fishes. Tiny free-swimming shrimplike crustaceans appear in huge numbers in the open seas and are a major part of the diet of many baleen whales.
Mammal	Any member of the taxonomic group of mammalia, which are warm blooded, have hair and nurse their young (whales, otters, and humans). They have nostrils, breath surface air, have a high metabolism, carry the fetus in the uterus, have milk-secreting glands to suckle their young, display complex patterns of reproduction and parental care.
Manta ray	A giant ray with winglike pectoral fins.
Marine	Of or found in the sea.
Marine Biologist	A professional who deals with the origin, history, characteristics and habits of plants and animals of the sea.
Marine Invertebrates	Animals that lack a spinal column and internal skeleton.
Matted	Thick tangle.
Meander	To take a winding course.
Metabolism	Physical and chemical changes within a living organism involved in the maintenance of life; the ongoing chemical and physical process in living organisms and cells, including the transformation of food into living tissue and living tissue into waste products and energy.
Migrate	To move to another region with the change of stimuli such as the seasons of the year.
Morsel	A small bite or portion of food.
Mussel	Any of the various bivalve mollusks of fresh or salt waters.
Octopus	A mollusk with a soft body and eight arms covered with suckers.
Opalescent	An iridescent silica of various colors; some varieties are semiprecious.
Orange cup coral	A hard skeleton secreted by certain marine polyps, reefs and atolls.
Orca	Another name for a killer whale.
Osmoregulation	A bodily system that maintains the salinity of body fluids within a narrow range of salt content, which is usually much lower than that of seawater. Sea animals must keep the osmotic concentration of their body fluids constant despite the saltwater environment. The system regulates fluids to create a balance in the body.

Osprey	(Pandion haliaetus)—a fish eater in the raptor family of birds. It lives near lakes, rivers, bays and coastal marshes. Its widespread wings are held in a distinctive "m" shape when observed from below.
Pectoral fins	Paired flippers; paddle-shaped forelimbs used for stability and steering.
Pelagic	Having to do with or living in the open sea or oceans; not associated with the seabed or coastal areas.
Pink sea anemones	A plant with cup-shaped flowers of white, pink, red, or purple.
Plankton	Plants and animals that swim weakly, or not at all, and drift with ocean currents; most are tiny.
Planktos	To drift or float at the whim of the current or swim only weakly; minute aquatic organisms that float or drift near the surface in the open sea, comprised of plant (phyotplankton) and animal (zooplankton) organisms.
Pod	A group of animals, such as whales, swimming or moving closely together; long-term social group of whales.
Prowl	To roam about in a stealthy or sneaky manner as during a search for prey.
Radar	Radio waves, as opposed to sound waves, used to detect the presence and distance of objects.
Raft	A large number of sea otters or sea lions together in the water; a group of sea otters gathered together in a permanent or temporary unit.
Refuge	Shelter or protection from danger during difficulty or present threat.
Respiratory	The action or process of breathing; the act of assimilating oxygen and releasing carbon dioxide and other respiratory byproducts via the lungs.
Sarcasm	A taunting or caustic remark, generally ironic.
Sea otters	(Enhydra lutris)—mammals of the Mustelidae family that bear and nurse living young, are meat eaters and have no anal scent glands. They are the only marine mammal that catches fish with its paws instead of its teeth. They love to eat shellfish, crabs, sea urchins and small fish. Sea otters have dense fur and weblike feet.
Sea urchin	A small sea animal with a round body in a shell covered with sharp spines.
Sinister	Threatening harm, evil.
Slough	Pronounced *slew,* a narrow, winding waterway of either salt or fresh water edged with muddy and marshy ground. Either open to, or separated from, the sea, such a coastal wetland has no year-round flow of fresh water—only in winter when the rain brings fresh water in from the adjacent hills. Plankton drifts through water currents, which are generally quiet with no waves. As the tide rises, seawater enters the slough, gently flooding its banks and extending further inland. Migratory birds such as snow egrets and blue herons typically rest in the treetops, refuel with food such as fat innkeeper worms before continuing a long journey. Leopard sharks, sea otters and bat rays swim in the slough searching for food.

Sonar	Emitted sound and its returning echo, with which ships and submarines detect the presence, distance and position of objects.
Songs	A complex pattern of low-frequency grunts, squeals, whistles, wails and chirps such as those produced by male humpback whales. The songs have predictable patterns and change over time.
Squid	A long, slender sea mollusk with eight arms and two long tentacles.
Stealthy	Secret action, movement under cover; difficult to detect.
Stipe	Stemlike portion of a kelp plant to which the blades (leafy portion) are connected.
Talon	The claw of a bird of prey.
Tubercles	Circular bumps on the surface of the skin along the flippers and dorsal fins of some cetaceans.
Thermoregulation	Natural temperature control in the body.
Triumphant	Successful, victorious.
Underfur	The inner fur layer of otters.
Unison	Performing the same motion or activity at the same time.
Ventilate	To circulate fresh air with an opening for the escape of air, gas and other filtered elements.
Zooplankton	Animal plankton including amphipods, copepods, isopods, krill, polychaetes and pteropods.

ANIMAL AND PLANT CLASSIFICATION

The Linnaeus taxonomical system classifies plants and animals according to similarities in structure, habits and function of their various parts. Living things are identified by: (1) kingdom, (2) phylum, (3) subphylum, (4) class, (5) order, (6) suborder, (7) family, (8) genus and (9) species. The largest groupings consist of the plant and animal kingdom. Plants use sunlight to produce food through their own leaf and root systems. They grow firmly in one spot and do not move on their own. Look through the classifications on the following page and find the living organism that represents a plant.

Animals cannot make their own food and they must consume food to survive. Those without backbones are invertebrates and include insects, worms, sponges, mollusks, starfish and crustaceans. Animals with backbones are vertebrates. Vertebrates are subdivided into classes based upon whether they have scales, feathers or hair and reproductive activities such as producing live young, laying eggs or producing milk for their young. Vertebrates include the following classes: reptiles, birds, mammals, fish and amphibians. The remaining groups become more specific in animal characteristics. The animals in this book are named from the classification list on the following page.

Common Name	Blue Shark	Blue Whale	Bottlenose Dolphin	Common Dolphin	Dall's Porpoise	Great White Shark
Species	glauca	musculus	truncates	delphis	dalli	carcharias
Genus	Prionace	Balaenoptera	Tursiops	Delphinus	Phocoenoides	Carcharodon
Family	Carcharhinidae	Balaenopterdae	Delphinidae	Delphinidae	Phocoenidae	Lamnidae
Suborder		Mysticetes	Odontocetes	Odontocetes	Odontocetes	
Order	Carcharhiniformes	Cetacea	Cetacea	Cetacea	Cetacea	Lamniformes
Class	Chondrichthyes	Mammalia	Mammalia	Mammalia	Mammalia	Chondrichthyes
Subphylum	Vertebrata	Vertebrata	Vertebrata	Vertebrata	Vertebrata	Vertebrata
Phylum	Chordata	Chordata	Chordata	Chordata	Chordata	Chordata
Kingdom	Animalia	Animalia	Animalia	Animalia	Animalia	Animalia

Common Name	Harbor Seal	Human Being	Humpback Whale	Kelp	Killer Whale	Leopard Shark
Species	vitulina	sapiens	novaeangliae	pyrifera	orca	semifasciata
Genus	Phoca	Homo	Megaptera	Macrocystis	Orcinus	Triakis
Family	Phocidae	Hominidae	Balaenopteridae	Laminariaceae	Delphinidae	Triakidae
Suborder			Mysticetes		Odontocetes	
Order	Pinnipedia	Primate	Cetacea	Laminariales	Cetacea	Caracharhiniformes
Class	Mammalia	Mammalia	Mammalia	Phaeophyceae	Mammalia	Chondrichthyes
Subphylum	Vertebrata	Vertebrata	Vertebrata		Vertebrata	Vertebrata
Phylum	Chordata	Chordata	Chordata	Phaeophyta	Chordata	Chordata
Kingdom	Animalia	Animalia	Animalia	Plantae	Animalia	Animalia

Common Name	Manta Ray	Osprey	Sea Lion	Sea Otter
Species	birostris	haliaetus	californianus	lutris
Genus	Manta	Pandion	Zalophus	Enhydra
Family	Myliobatidae	Pandionidae	Otariidae	Mustelidae
Suborder				Fissipedia
Order	Myliobatiformes	Falconiformes	Pinnipedia	Carnivora
Class	Chondrichthyes	Aves	Mammalia	Mammalia
Subphylum	Vertebrata	Vertebrata	Vertebrata	Vertebrata
Phylum	Chordata	Chordata	Chordata	Chordata
Kingdom	Animalia	Animalia	Animalia	Animalia

ANSWER KEY

FIND HIDDEN WORDS

CROSSWORD PUZZLE

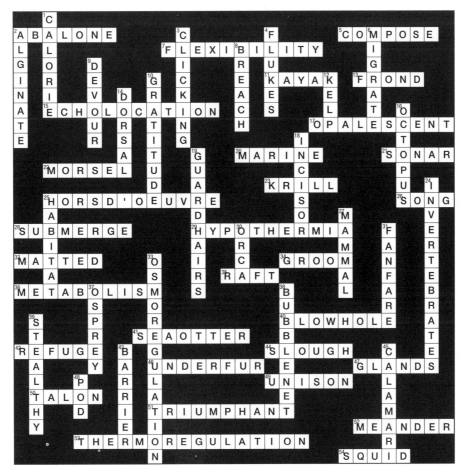

What Am I Answer Key:

1. Great White Shark   2. Blue Shark   3. Leopard Shark   4. Humpback Whale   5. Bottlenose Dolphin
6. Killer Whale   7. Giant Kelp   8. Sea Otter   9. Sea Lion   10. Osprey   11. Giant Manta Ray

Word Scramble Answer Key:

1. O T T E R
     6 4

2. B R E A C H
  12   3 13

3. F L U K E S
  10 7   5 6

4. H A B I T A T
    2   9   14

5. K A Y A K
  3 15 3

6. A B A L O N E
  3   7 11 6

7. O R C A
     3

8. O S P R E Y
  1 8   6

9. S L O U G H
  1 7   2

10. S Q U I D
   1   9

Message:

S H A R K S   H E L P   S E A   L I F E   S T A Y   I N   B A L A N C E
1 2 3 4 5   1 2 6 7 8   1 6 3   7 9 10 6   1 14 3 15   9 11   12 3 7 3 11 13 6

OT's Detective Activity Answer Key:

1. Hydra and Muste prefer to eat invertebrates. Clams and sea urchins are invertebrates. Hydra prefers to eat animals that eat kelp and we know that sea urchins love to eat kelp, therefore Hydra prefers to eat sea urchins. The remaining invertebrate is the clam, which Muste prefers to eat.

2. Nova prefers to eat fish that become confused by bubbles. Bubbles confuse herring, therefore Nova prefers herring.

3. Bottlenose prefers to eat fish in alphabetical order. Since anchovies start with "a", Bottlenose prefers anchovies. Also answer 4 determines the smallest fish, which is the anchovies.

4. Osprey Talons prefers to eat the largest fish. Since sardines are larger than anchovies but smaller than herring, which is not the largest fish, the only remaining fish is the salmon. Based on this clue, the anchovies would be smallest, then the sardines, then the herring and the largest would be the only remaining fish, the salmon. Since OT prefers the largest fish, it would be the salmon.

5. Zalo prefers to eat fish. The only remaining fish for Zalo would be the sardines.

6. Orcin prefers to eat sea mammals. There are only two sea mammals, the harbor seal and elephant seal, which has more blubber. Since Carcha prefers the sea mammal with more blubber, the elephant seal, the only remaining sea mammal Orcin would prefer could be the harbor seal.

Memory Fun Answer Key:

1. a,c,d
2. c,d,e
3. yes, reduces competition for the same food
4. a,b,c,d
5. b
6. b
7. a
8. 1) Nova, 2) Bottlenose, 3) Charlie and Carla, 4) Orcin, 5) Zalo, 6) OT, 7) Carcha
9. d
10. d
11. b
12. True
13. True
14. a) hypothermia, b) echolocation, c) thermoregulation, d) osmoregulation, e) metabolism
15. d
16. a,b,c,d
17. True, because of their loose skeleton and absence of a collarbone
18. a,b,c
19. press water with forepaws; blow air into skin; shaking, scrubbing, or licking fur
20. a,b,c
21. False, because only two otters can make a raft
22. a) dorsal fin, b) flukes, c) pectoral fin, d) blowhole, e) tubercles
23. a,b,c,d
24. True, respiratory system (large lungs and flexible ribs) delivers oxygen under water pressure
25. False, otters have a special lens and crystals in both eyes to accommodate low levels of light
26. a,b
27. No, only at the surface
28. a) Bottlenose, b) Carcha, c) Orcin, d) Nova, e) OT, f) Zalo, g) Muste
29. c
30. True, progressively lengthened toes help otters swim more efficiently
31. a
32. a) 2, b) 1, c) 1, d) hopefully likes
33. a,b,c,d,e
34. a,b,c,d,
35. a,b,c,d
36. b, because sonar uses sound to find objects; echolocation uses clicks to find objects
37. c, because "Orcin" is a killer whale and "Nova" is a humpback whale
38. a, because Carcha eats seal lions; Muste eats abalone
39. False, because killer whales use a stealthy visual sense
40. d
41. a) eek, b) bark, c) bellow, d) squeak, e) squawk, f) spouted
42. b, because calamari is cooked squid; steamed clams are cooked clams
43. b
44. a) red octopus, b) Carcha, c) OT, d) Nova, e) Muste/Hydra, f) Bottlenose
45. True, because it usually means poisonous or toxic
46. d
47. False, because their thick fur can cause heat prostration in a unventilated area
48. a, b, c
49. a,b,c
50. b, because otters create a water barrier when their ears are back while they are under the water
51. a) Nova, b) Delphi, c) OT, d) Bottlenose, e) Zalo, f) Orcin and pod
52. a) Orcin and pod, b) Triak, c) OT, d) Biros, e) blue heron, f) Conch, g) Carcha
53. They both like rafts!
54. Will you groom me?

Cryptic Message of the Kelp Forest Answer Key:

Sea otters help protect the kelp forest by eating the sea invertebrates that feed on the kelp.

Create Words Answer Key:

Adieu, admit, adult, aid, aide, AIDS, ail, aim, aisle, ale, alms, alum, am, amid, amide, amulet, amuse, as, aside, at, ate, audit, autism, dais, dale, dam, dame, damsel, date, datum, deal, deem, deism, delta, demise, detail, dial, die, diesel, dilate, dilute, dismal, distal, dual, due, duel, duet, dust, ease, easel, east, eat, edema, edit, elate, elide, elite, elm, else, elude, e-mail, emit, emu, emulate, étude, id, idea, ideal, ides, idle, Islam, isle, islet, it, item, its, lad, laid, lam, lame, last, late, laud, lea, lead, lease, least, led, lee, lees, lei, lest, let, lid, lie, lieu, lime, limeade, list, litmus, lust, lute, mad, made, maid, mail, male, malt, mast, mat, mate, maul, me, mead, meal, meat, medal, media, medial, mediate, medium, meet, meld, melt, mesa, metal, mete, midst, mild, mile, milt, misdeal, mist, mite, mu, mud, mule, muse, must, mute, sad, said, sail, salt, salute, same, sate, sea, seal, seat, sedate, see, seed, seem , set, side, sidle, sild, silt, simulate, sit, site, slam, slat, sled, sleet, slide, slim slit, slue, slum, smelt, smile, smite, smut, stadium, staid, stale, stead, steal, steam, steed, steel, stem, stile, stud, sue, suede, suet, suit, sum, tad, tail, tale, tame, tau, tea, teal, team ,tease, teasel, tedium, tee, teem, tidal, tide, tie, tilde, tile, time, times, tumid, use, used

MAZE

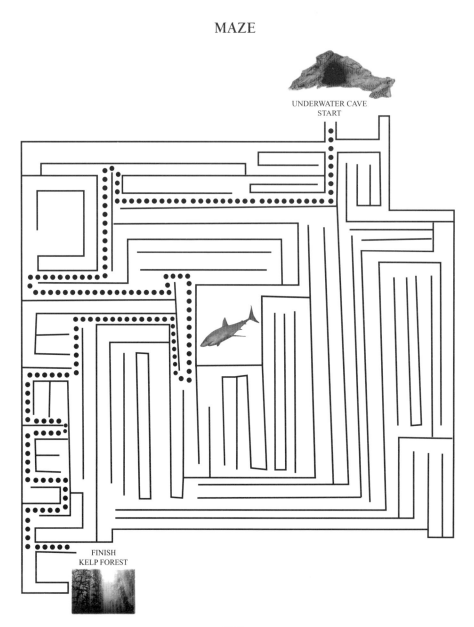

101

The author wishes to thank the following individuals for their contributions to this story:

Sydney Ann Fischer, Illustrator

Sydney Fischer is an illustrator living and working in California. She studied fine art at the University of Michigan in Ann Arbor and illustration and design at Kendall College of Art and Design in Grand Rapids. Sydney taught conceptual illustration at San Jose State University. Her work is nationally and internationally recognized, winning numerous awards including honors from the Denver Art Directors Club and the Society of Newspaper Design.

Philip Sammet, Underwater Photographer & Diving Instructor

Philip Sammet assisted the author in obtaining the surface photographs of the otters used in this book. He also provided nitrox training and enhanced the diving skills of the author. Phil and his wife, Kim, reside in Monterey where Phil teaches all levels of diving from nitrox to trimix and rebreather at the consumer and instructor level. On weekends he is the captain of the dive boat Cypress Point—a 65-foot vessel, transporting divers around Monterey, Carmel and Big Sur. Phil holds a 100-ton masters license and also serves as an emergency medical technician and a hyperbaric technician. Throughout the years, he has worked on many film projects for organizations such as the BBC, PBS Nature, NHK, Discovery Channel, and IMAX Films. Phil also works part time for MBARI aboard the Western Flyer—the finest research vessel of its kind. Phil's wife, Kim, who appeared with Phil in the kayak photograph within the story, is a registered nurse and hyperbaric nurse working at the local decompression chamber. They were recently blessed with the birth of a beautiful baby girl, Rachael.

Jill S. Eastwood, Editor

Following 25 years in Corporate America, supporting the top echelon within some of the largest companies in this country, Jill Eastwood now devotes her full time to serving as a literary editor for independent authors, researchers and graduate students worldwide. The expertise she has developed over the years in various industries and fields allows her to effectively support authors within all disciplines. She also serves as a technical editor for companies throughout California's Silicon Valley. Her work is highly valued and sought from around the world.

Mary Jane Adams, Underwater Photographer

Scuba diving and underwater photography have been the favorite hobbies of Mary Jane Adams since 1975. Although she resides in Southern California, most of her diving adventures have taken place in the tropical Indo-Pacific. She swam with many beautiful, exotic fish and many species of sharks. In all her years of diving, a shark has never threatened her. Mary Jane has photographed many species of sharks underwater without the use of protective cages; however, the great white shark pictures in this book were shot from the safety of a steel cage. On a special expedition in South Australia to find and photograph these large predators, Mary Jane spent days chumming the sea with blood and chopped fish to coax the great white sharks within camera range. The worldwide threat that overfishing presents to the shark population is of great concern to this photographer. Mary Jane is convinced of the important role these animals play in marine ecology.

Andy Sallmon, Underwater & Nature Photographer

Andy Sallmon, a freelance underwater and nature photographer, specializes in images of marine life and the overall marine environment. His images have been displayed in natural-history museums, art galleries, hotels and private collections. They have also been used for advertising by various organizations in their brochures, catalogs, websites and magazines. Andy leads underwater photographic tours to remote destinations along the western Pacific coast from Alaska to Mexico. He is known best by the hundreds of amateur photographers who have attended his classes and seminars focused on underwater photography. His photographic credits include images printed in the following publications: the American MPC CD Rom Amazing Marine Life, Lonely Planet Guide to Diving and Snorkeling Hawaii, Lonely Planet Guide to Oahu, Discover Diving Magazine and Skin Diver Magazine. Andy taught underwater photography to the author of this story. His beautiful surface and underwater pictures are used throughout the book.

Sue Hale, Editor

Sue Hale taught English for many years in San Jose, California, along with her involvement in theater productions. Sue edited the initial draft of this book; however, her illnesses prevented her from continuing the project. She recently passed away and much sorrow is felt in her absence. The author deeply regrets that Sue will not see the end of the otter story, but she indeed lives on through its pages.

PHOTOGRAPH AND ILLUSTRATION CREDITS

Front Cover Photograph Andy Sallmon © 2001

Front Inside Cover Photograph Andy Sallmon © 2001

Page 1, 19, 24, 26, 28, 34, 38, 40, 46 Photographs: George Kingston

Page 48, 49, 50, 51, 52, 66, 67, 68, 70, 72 Photographs: George Kingston

Page 2, 4, 6, 8, 10, 12, 21, 39, 63 Photographs Andy Sallmon © 2001

Page 13, 14, 29, 30, 31, 32, 35, 36, 59, 60 Border Illustrations: George Kingston

Page 15, 18, 22, 37, 42, 53, 58 Illustrations: Sydney Fischer

Page 16, 33, 43, 45, 47, 62, 64 Illustrations: George Kingston

Page 32 Song: George Kingston

Page 55, 57 Photographs Mary Jane Adams © 2001

Page 60 Song: George Kingston

Back Inside Cover Photograph Andy Sallmon © 2001

Back Cover Photograph: George Kingston